THE ALASKA MOTHER GOOSE

and other north country nursery rhymes

By SHELLEY GILL • Illustrations by SHANNON CARTWRIGHT

Printed on recycled paper

Second Printing September 1987
Third Printing July 1988
Fourth Printing November 1988
Fifth Printing February 1990

Paws IV Publishing Company
P.O. Box 2364
Homer, Alaska 99603

Library of Congress number: 87-060489
ISBN 0-934007-02-0 (pb)
ISBN 0-934007-05-5 (hc)

Sixth Printing January 1991
Seventh Printing January 1992

Dedicated
to

My mother, Caroline, who gave me a love of words.
S.G.

and

My parents
Marceline and Charles
who taught me to see.
S.C.

Snow goose, snow gander
fly away home.
Spring light has dawned
from Whitehorse to Nome.

Hi diddle dare
the moose and the bear
danced by the light
of the moon.
The lynx did a jig
while the seal took a swig
and the owl and the shrew
sang a tune.

The portly tufted puffin
waddles in the sand:
A plump and shy old parrot,
he's clumsy on the land.

But when he tips into the sea,
he flaps his wings and flies,
chasing fish beneath the waves
'cross salty seaweed skies.

The crane's ballet:
on spindle legs she glides,
dancing at the edge
of the evening tide.

The bear cub spied
some ducklings at play,
splashing and swimming
on a sunny spring day.
He paddled out
and joined their parade.
What a silly sight
the bear cub made!

Spruce for breakfast,
birch for lunch,
but willows are
a beaver's brunch.

From rocky dens
a marmot trill
whistles warning 'cross the hill.
Hide and seek
when shadows glide,
he takes a peek then scoots inside.

In Kodiak Harbor
the sea otter floats,
surrounded by buoys
and fishing boats.
Munching on urchins
with feet in the air,
watching the seagulls
he hasn't a care.

Said the raven to the flea,
"Come out and see the sun!
It's dark in there,
in a musk ox's hair.
Come out and
have some fun!"
"Oh no," said the flea,
"You can't trick me!
I'll stay in here
and sneak a peek,
and stay away
from your big black beak!"

On cliffs of granite
'cross rocks so steep,
travels a band
of white dall sheep.
Carefully they step,
gently they leap
over schist and shale,
their footing to keep.

Mossberries, crowberries,
blackberries too;
Make the black bears'
teeth turn blue.

Beware the stalks
    and yellow spines
prickly as
    a porcupine.
The devil's club-
    a plant to fear,
with shiny leaves
    and wicked spears.

Beneath a patch of fireweed
another world's in bloom–
Where hungry lemmings gather seeds
to store in tiny rooms;
The ground squirrel nibbles nutmeat
in his grassy little nest.
Then cold winds howl and he burrows deep
to get his winter rest.

Old wolverine is very cross,
as he sulks in his bed of reindeer moss.
In a stinky swamp his day was spent,
now he's lost his musky scent.

The whale and the walrus
splash and slide,
surfing in the ocean tide.
As icy floes drift around
they dive and dance
in an arctic playground.

Porcupine, porcupine, sat on a log,
porcupine fell in a cranberry bog.

The silver salmon
leap through the air
missing the claws
of the big brown bear.
They flick their tails
at the angry boar,
then splash away
from his mighty roar.

Joy to leap at falling leaves,
to sniff the fresh peeled bark.

Joy to howl beneath the moon;
to chase the herd at dark.

Snow goose, snow gander
fly on, fly on.
Autumn is flaming,
it's time you were gone!

North they race
with heads thrown high,
a thousand hooves
come clicking by.
A herd so large,
a herd so vast,
the tundra trembles
when caribou pass.

The misty dusk settles
'round a gold harvest moon.
Piercing the silence
comes the cry of the loon.
Fall leaves grow brittle;
crisp comes the night.
The north land glows, quiet,
in autumn's rose light.

Old bull moose who dreamed he could fly
sailed across a starry sky.
But when daylight came he was up a tree:
A peculiar place for a moose to be!

As the hair seal rose,
he spotted the nose
and ducked beneath the ice.

You foolish brute,
hide your snoot
or your tummy pays the price!

Fox be nimble
hare be quick,
race through willows
on ice so slick.

Dip and dodge,
leap and strain,
then burrow home
safe again.

Twinkle, twinkle
Northern Lights,
sparkle in the
arctic night.
Up above the clouds so high,
blue-green ribbons
in the sky.

Twinkle, twinkle
Northern Lights,
shimmer in my
dreams tonight.

GLOSSARY

Marmots usually live in an underground burrow beneath a jumble of rocks. When two marmots meet, they often touch noses or wrestle in a friendly fashion. They are early to bed, early to rise critters, often spending the day sunning on rocks. They are terrific whistlers who can also bark, yip and yell.

Snow geese are one of many different varieties of geese migrating north in early spring. There are probably less than 200 pairs of snow geese nesting in Alaska.

Black bears have terrible eyesight but a keen sense of hearing and smell. Black bears eat fish, berries, plants and meat.

Musk oxen, known by the Eskimos as "omingmak" or "the bearded ones," will line up like so many covered wagons forming a circle around their young to defend them from predators.

A sticky customer, the porcupine is also known as the hedge hog, porky or quill pig.

Sea otters never eat on land, preferring to float on their backs and munch on a variety of sea delicacies. They will often crack two clams together or even balance a rock on their chest and smash the clam against it to expose the rich meat.

Wolves live in packs and spend a lot of time playing games with each other when they aren't hunting or sleeping. They leap joyfully to catch falling autumn leaves, slide on their bellies in the snow and chase their tails. Fighting is very uncommon.

Arctic (white) fox are sometimes described as blue fox when they enter the summer color phase. Likewise, red fox are often described by colors such as cross, silver and black.

Snowshoe hare have large, well-furred hind feet that allow them to scamper on top of deep snow as if they were on snowshoes.

Collared lemmings are the only rodents to turn white in the winter. They race through a tangle of trails beneath the snow and eat grass, sedges and even insects.

Clumsy in the air, the tufted puffin or sea parrot is built for diving and swimming underwater. Puffins flap their wings for propellsion and use their webbed feet as rudders.

Newborn caribou calves can walk within an hour and, after a few days, outrun a man or swim across rivers and lakes.

Brown bears can live 20 years in the wild. The male bear is called a boar. Family ties are strong and the mothers (sows) are very protective. Sometimes a sow will adopt as many as six other cub orphans.

Mossberries, crowberries and blackberries are different names for the same berry.

Silver or coho's are one of five varieties of salmon that spawn in the north country. Others are the chinook (king), the humpy (pink), the dog (chum) and the sockeye (red).

Lynx or "link" kittens have a cry like a falcon that they use to call their mother when they wander too far from the den.

Wolverine or "devil bears" have a prized fur for Indian parka ruffs because their long guard hairs will not accumulate frost. They are very canny and have been known to follow traplines, remove every bit of bait, every trapped animal, then destroy or hide the traps.

Polar bears capture ringed seals by waiting for them at breathing holes or at the edge of leads or cracks in the ice. Legend says they cover their black noses with their white paws so the seals won't spot them, but biologists say this is just a myth.